Coyote &

The Quail • Horned Toad • His Bow • Skunk • Turkey • Rabbit • The Mice • Locust • The Rock • Bluebird • The Blackbirds • The Rattlesnake • The Turtle

Native American Folk Tales
retold by Joe Hayes

A Mariposa Book

Illustrations by Lucy Jelinek

Published by
Mariposa Publishing
922 Baca Street
Santa Fe, New Mexico 87501
(505) 988-5582

SECOND EDITION
FIRST PRINTING 1983

"The Day It Snowed Tortillas" by Joe Hayes and "Coyote &" by Joe Hayes also available on Cassette tape by
Have Stories Will Travel, 700 Amherst N.E., Albuquerque, NM 87106, (505) 268-4601.

ISBN # 0-93553-01-3

for James Hayes,
the first storyteller
I ever heard.

JH

for Myra Jelinek,
who has always
encouraged me.

LJ

Coyote &

TABLE OF CONTENTS

INTRODUCTION

Many American Indian stories are sacred. They are part of the religion of the people who tell them, and so belong to just one tribe or sometimes just a part of the tribe. Sometimes Coyote plays a role in these religious stories.

But the coyote stories in this collection are different. They are told for entertainment. They are especially loved by children, who delight in Coyote's foolish antics.

And these stories do not belong to any single tribe. Most of them can be found among Native American peoples throughout the West. Of course, they change from one tribe to another—or even from one storyteller to another in the same tribe.

So each story has many versions. And the version in this book won't exactly match any that was collected from Indian storytellers. These are my own retellings. They are a combination of the inspiration of the old stories and the imagination of the storyteller.

Some important collections which helped me create these retellings are listed at the back of this book. Most were made many years ago, when a rich supply of stories still existed in the people's memories.

Finally, you may be confused by Coyote in these stories. Is he an animal or is he a man? Grenville Goodwin, who collected Apache stories in the 1930's asked the Indian storytellers, "How do you think of the animals when you are telling or listening to these stories? Was Coyote like he is today, or did he look like a man?"

One said, "I think of him being just like a man when I tell about him, with face, hands and feet like a man. They say that all animals were people in those days."

Another answered, "The old people used to say that Coyote wore clothes in the stories, but that he walked on all fours and had the body of a coyote. So that is the way I think of him."

So let your imagination picture Coyote however it wants to. Whether he looks like a man or an animal, I hope he'll make you chuckle with his pranks. And maybe once or twice he'll even make you laugh at yourself!

Coyote &
His Bow

From the stories about Coyote, we can see that if he wouldn't always try to be so clever, he might not end up being so foolish. But he'll probably never change, for he's been the same since the beginning of time.

In the beginning, when all the animals had first been made, no animal was more useful or more fierce than any other. They were all equal.

Then one day, the Sky God called First Man to him and told First Man to make many bows and arrows — as many as there were kinds of animals. No two bows and arrows should be exactly the same size.

Then First Man must give one bow and arrow to each animal — the biggest to the animal who would be fiercest, the second biggest to the second most fierce, and so on. The smallest bow and arrow would go to the least powerful of all the animals.

So First Man set to work. And as he worked, Coyote kept snooping around to see what he was doing. Coyote figured out the meaning of First Man's work, and he wanted to receive the largest bow and arrow. So he began to plot in his mind.

First Man worked day and night without stopping and on the ninth day he finished the last bow. That evening First Man called all the animals together and told them to sleep through the night in that spot. In the morning he would give out the bows and arrows he had made.

All the animals lay down to sleep as they had been told—all, that is, but Coyote. Coyote just lay with his head on his paws and pretended to sleep, because he had a plan. He would stay awake all night and be the first to run to meet First Man in the morning. That way he would receive the biggest bow.

But as the night dragged on, Coyote grew very sleepy. He knew that if he stayed lying down, he would fall asleep. He got up and walked around. But he grew even more sleepy. So he began to dance.

Then Bear began to grumble in his sleep and Badger stretched as if he were about to wake up, so Coyote had to stop dancing. He certainly didn't want to wake any of the other animals.

Coyote sat staring at the moon with his eyes wide open. If he could sing, that would keep him awake. But he didn't dare. Still, the bright light in his eyes should help. Then, late at night, the moon set.

Coyote was desperate. It couldn't be long now till sunrise. The morning star had already risen. But his eyelids felt heavy as rocks. He couldn't hold them open.

So Coyote found two short sticks and with them he propped his eyes open. He felt very pleased with that idea. He lay down facing the east, thinking that even if he fell asleep, the sun shining into his open eyes would wake him.

But no sooner had Coyote lain down than he fell fast asleep. *Pop!* His eyes snapped shut, and the sticks jabbed through his eyelids and fastened them together!

The eastern sky grew gray with the dawn. The sun rose. And all the animals went forth to meet First Man — that is, all except Coyote. He lay snoring with his eyes locked shut, dreaming of how he would enjoy being the most powerful animal of all.

First Man gave the longest bow to Mountain Lion, and he became the fiercest, most respected of all the animals. The second longest went to Bear. Each animal received a bow, until there was only one left — the smallest of all.

First Man and the animals looked around, wondering who was missing. And they saw Coyote.

They all ran to where Coyote lay sleeping and danced around him pointing and laughing. Some of them jumped up and down on Coyote's back.

Coyote yawned and stretched and struggled to his feet. But he couldn't open his eyes. They were held shut by those sticks.

First Man pulled the sticks from Coyote's eyelids—*plip! plip!* And he gave Coyote the smallest bow and arrow. Coyote was very disappointed.

But First Man told him, "Coyote, don't be sad. It's true you won't be very fierce. Neither am I. But like me you are very clever, and that must be enough for us to get along in this world."

And it has been. But if Coyote would use his cleverness a bit more wisely, he might get along a lot better!

Coyote & Skunk

Coyote is a hunter. But he isn't very good at it. Every time you see him he's scrawny and looks as though he hasn't had a good meal in months. But have you ever noticed Skunk? He doesn't call himself a hunter, but he's always plump and well fed.

One day Coyote was lying under a bush wishing he had a nice fat rabbit or some juicy prairie dogs to eat. But he didn't feel like going to all the work it took to catch one of those animals.

As he lay there wondering if there wasn't an easier way to get a meal, he saw Skunk go waddling past toward the arroyo. Skunk was fat, and he couldn't run fast, but Coyote had found out the hard way what would happen if he tried to make a meal of Skunk. His eyes still watered when he remembered how they had stung when Skunk had sprayed him in the face.

Just then, a plan sprang into Coyote's head. He trotted over to Skunk and sat down in front of him.

"Skunk," said Coyote, "wouldn't you like to eat some roast prairie do[for a change?"

Skunk was an unfriendly fellow. He just muttered, "Oh, leave me alone. I'm doing fine already."

But Coyote coaxed, "Come on, Skunk. You must get tired of eating bird's eggs and grubs from under rocks. Wouldn't you like to sink your teeth into some nice sweet prairie dog meat?"

No one liked a good meal better than fat little Skunk. He began to get interested. Coyote went on, "I can already hear those plump little prairie dogs sizzling over the fire now. *Hhmm-mmm!* And what a delicious smell they give off as they roast! How about it, Skunk? Shall I tell you my plan?"

Skunk's mouth was watering. He couldn't remember the last time he'd had roast prairie dog. He listened to Coyote's plan.

Then Skunk shuffled off down the bank of the arroyo. When Skunk had disappeared around a bend, Coyote started singing and doing his rain dance. Dark clouds gathered above him and rain poured down.

The dry arroyo began to flow. Soon it was a gushing river, and Coyote threw himself into the water and floated downstream.

Skunk was waiting around the bend. He caught Coyote by the tail as he floated along and dragged him halfway up the bank. Coyote lay there motionless, his fur all matted and caked with mud.

Coyote let his mouth hang open with his long pink tongue dangling out onto the dirt. And Skunk went to some nearby grass and picked little white seeds to put in Coyote's ears and eyes and at the corner of his mouth, as though flies had been laying eggs on him. Coyote looked quite dead.

Then Skunk padded off to the prairie dog village. He thumped his foot on the ground and called out, "Come and see! Come and see! Coyote is dead! Coyote is dead!"

The prairie dogs peeked from their holes, but they didn't believe Skunk. "Coyote can't be dead!" they chirped. "Coyote can't be dead! Coyote's medicine is strong. Coyote can't be dead!"

But Skunk kept on, "Come and see! Send a scout to look for you. Your enemy is dead!"

And so the fastest prairie dog ran to the arroyo and saw Coyote. He brought back the word. "It's true! It's true! Coyote has drowned. Flies are laying eggs on his dead body!"

Then all the prairie dogs cheered. And Skunk told them, "Come. You must do your victory dance around his body. I will drum for you."

They all hurried to where Coyote lay and and while Skunk drummed with his hind foot, the prairie dogs danced around Coyote singing their victory song.

"Sing loud!" Skunk urged them. "Raise your faces and sing to the sky!"

When the prairie dogs raised their faces skyward, Skunk spun around and sent his spray into the air. It fell in the prairie dogs' eyes. They squealed and clutched their faces with their paws.

And Skunk cried, "Now, Coyote! Jump up and get our meal."

Coyote leaped up and began grabbing prairie dogs. Skunk rolled on the ground laughing. What a pile of prairie dogs they would have to roast for supper!

Together Coyote and Skunk dug a trench in the ground and built a fire in it. When the fire had burned down to coals, they set the prairie dogs on to roast. They covered the prairie dogs with dirt, leaving just the tails sticking out, then lay down to rest until dinner was ready.

A delicious smell drifted up from the roasting prairie dogs, and Coyote's stomach started to growl. "Mmmmm!" he thought, "I could eat all those prairie dogs myself, I'm so hungry."

Then another plan came into Coyote's mind. "Skunk," Coyote said. "Why don't we have some fun to pass the time until our meal is ready. Let's run a race to that far mesa and back."

Skunk sniffled, "No, I'm no runner. You know that."

But Coyote told him, "You can run as well as anyone, Skunk. You've just never tried. You can probably beat me."

"What if I could? Why would anyone want to run a race? I'm happy just lying here in the shade."

That was what Coyote wanted to hear. "I'll give you a reason to race," he told Skunk. "We'll make a bet. We'll say that the one who wins the race can eat *all* the prairie dogs! So when you beat me, you'll get all the prairie dogs for yourself!"

Skunk rolled over and looked at Coyote. "You'll have to give me a head start," he insisted.

Coyote wasn't worried about beating Skunk. "Of course you can have a head start. You can go clear to that bush. See it? It's almost half way to the mesa. Go on. I'll start when you reach the bush."

So Skunk waddled off toward the bush and Coyote waited. When Skunk reached the bush, he saw a badger hole under it and he shuffled down into the hole.

Soon Coyote came racing past. Then Skunk came out of the hole and went back to the fire. He dug up all the prairie dogs and cut off their tails. Then he piled the dirt back over the coals and stuck the prairie dog tails into the mound.

Skunk carried his supper off to a nearby ledge and began to eat.

Meanwhile Coyote was still running. He reached the mesa without seeing any sign of Skunk. "That fat little fellow is faster than I thought," Coyote said to himself. He turned and ran back even faster.

Coyote still hadn't passed Skunk when he reached the fire again, but he saw the mound of dirt still in place over the coals and the prairie dog tails sticking out. He thought, "Skunk must have lost his way. Oh, well, that's his problem. Now I'll have my supper!"

Coyote grabbed one of the tails and pulled. It came out in his paw. "Look at that!" he cried. "The tail comes right off when I pull it. These prairie dogs are well cooked!" He pulled another. And another. Then he dug the dirt away.

Coyote's forehead wrinkled. Where were the prairie dogs? Then something hit him on the head—*plunk!* He looked around and saw that it was a prairie dog bone.

Coyote looked up and saw Skunk on the ledge. "Skunk," Coyote pleaded. "Throw down a prairie dog—please!"

But Skunk only laughed. "No, Coyote. You get to eat just what you thought I would be eating—prairie dog bones!"

And Skunk stayed up on the ledge until he had eaten every one of the prairie dogs. Coyote had to be content with the bones Skunk threw down to him.

And so Coyote went away as lean and hungry as usual. And Skunk was as round and fat as he always is!

Coyote & Turkey

One day Coyote was hungry and thought he'd see if he could catch a rabbit or ground squirrel. He was loping through a small woods, heading for the open prairie, when he happened to look up and see a wild turkey sitting in a tree.

Coyote stopped and hollered up at the big bird, "Turkey! I see you up there. You may as well come down and let me eat you. If you don't, I'll climb the tree and get you. And don't try flying to another tree. I'll just knock that tree down and catch you anyway!"

Now those were just lies. Coyote couldn't do either of those things. But the foolish turkey believed those lies. He began to blubber and cry and plead for his life.

Then Coyote told an even bigger lie. "Whatever you do, Turkey, don't fly out onto the prairie. I have no power to harm anything on the prairie. And I want to eat you!"

Now Turkey laughed to himself, "Yuk-yuk-yuk — Coyote just told me how I can save myself." He spread his wings and flew out across the prairie.

Coyote ran along under the turkey. At first the bird was so high Coyote thought he'd lose him. But turkeys can't fly far and soon he began to drop down closer to the ground.

As soon as Turkey landed, Coyote pounced on him. And that was the end of that foolish bird. Coyote began his supper.

Now, Coyote is a cautious animal, and from time to time as he ate he would look up from the corner of his eye to make sure no harm was coming his way. Once when he glanced up to the left, Coyote saw a man with a raised club, about to strike him!

Coyote bolted and ran off as fast as he could. After he had run quite a distance, he looked to the left again, and there was the man, still right beside him with his club ready to strike Coyote.

Coyote ran farther this time, but again when he looked to the left, the man was next to him. Again and again Coyote ran. Then he tried dodging back and forth. Nothing helped. The man stayed right with him.

Coyote threw all his strength into his legs and ran his very fastest.

He ran until he collapsed. Then he rolled over onto his back and covered his face with his paws, begging the man not to kill him.

But when Coyote put his paws to his face, something snapped by his left eye. He looked at his paw, and there he held a big turkey feather that had been stuck to the fur beside his eye. That's what had looked like a man with a club!

Coyote was very embarrassed to think he had fled in panic from a feather. He slinked home. When he got there, and his wife saw the shape he was in, she asked what had happened.

Then Coyote told the biggest lie of all. "I got into an argument with a mountain lion and challenged him to a fight. But that big coward ran away. I had to chase him a long way, but I finally caught him and gave him a good beating!"

But Coyote did learn a lesson from that experience. To this day, whenever Coyote sees a human coming toward him, he always starts away at a trot—I'm sure you've seen him do that. That's because he's afraid he may have to run a long distance and wants to save his energy.

And have you noticed that he doesn't run straight away, but crosses in front of you at an angle, looking back over his shoulder? That's because he wants to be sure it's really a person and that he's not just running away from another feather!

Coyote & Rabbit

One morning Coyote went hunting and was lucky enough to see Rabbit sitting beside his hole half asleep. Coyote pounced on Rabbit and caught him around the neck with both paws.

Coyote laughed, "Ha-ha! Rabbit, I'm going to make a good meal of you!"

Rabbit was surprised, but he quickly recovered his wits. He told Coyote, *"Shhhhh!* Be quiet. He'll hear you and shoot us both!"

Coyote hadn't expected Rabbit to say that. He was puzzled. "Who?" Coyote asked.

"That man," Rabbit told Coyote. "Didn't you see him pass this way with his gun?"

Now Coyote was worried. He didn't want to get caught off guard by the man. Coyote looked around. "I don't see him."

"He passed right by here just a little while ago."
Rabbit trembled as he spoke. "I was so frightened I
shook all over." And to show what he was talking
about, Rabbit shook himself so violently that Coyote
was startled.

Coyote's grip around Rabbit's
neck loosened just enough
for Rabbit to jerk free.

He ran off as fast as he could.

Coyote was right behind Rabbit as he ran dodging across the desert. It was hard to tell who would win. But suddenly Rabbit saw another hole and turning sharply he dashed into it.

Coyote called down the hole, "Come out of there, Rabbit. If you don't, I'll dig you out!"

Of course Rabbit didn't come out, so Coyote began to dig away at the hole. But soon he grew tired. Coyote sat down to think. There must be a better way to get Rabbit out.

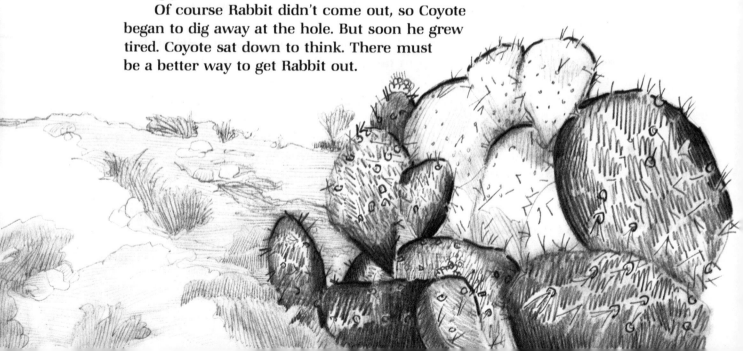

He got an idea. "Rabbit, you may as well come out right now," Coyote shouted, "because I'm going to build a fire and smoke you out!"

Rabbit called out of the hole, "What will you build your fire with, Coyote?"

Coyote looked around. "I'll build it with grass."

Rabbit laughed, "He-he-he. Grass? Don't you know that grass is my friend? It feeds me and lets me hide in it. The grass won't smoke me out."

Coyote had seen Rabbit eating grass, and several times Rabbit had escaped from him by hiding in tall grass. It must be true that grass was Rabbit's friend.

Coyote looked around again. "I'll get wood from cottonwood trees down by the river."

"Cottonwood trees?" Rabbit said. "They shade me and let me dig my holes among their roots. They are my friends too."

Coyote wouldn't give up. "I'll get sap from piñon trees, then."

Now Rabbit cried, "Oh, no! Don't do that. The piñon is no friend of mine!"

So Coyote ran about gathering a big ball of piñon pitch. He placed it in the entrance to the hole and with his fire drill he set it aflame.

The pitch began to melt and bubble and give off an inky black smoke as it burned. Coyote fanned the smoke into the hole.

Rabbit coughed, "Don't do that, Coyote. You're blowing smoke down here. I can't breathe!"

Coyote laughed gleefully. "That's just what I want to do." He put his mouth close to the flames and blew. More smoke went into the hole.

"Stop, Coyote," Rabbit gasped. "Stop blowing!"

Oh! Coyote was enjoying this. He put his muzzle right next to the burning puddle of pitch and blew as hard as he could.

Suddenly Rabbit spun around and with his hind feet kicked the burning pine tar right into Coyote's face.

Coyote howled in pain and jumped back. His muzzle was covered with sticky hot pitch. He rolled over pawing his face, but the fiery sap just burned his paws.

Coyote raced off to the river and thrust his whole head under water.

When he pulled his head out of the water, Coyote saw some choke cherries growing at the stream's edge and decided they would make a better breakfast than Rabbit anyway.

He ate his fill of the fruit and then went on his way. But to this day Coyote's nose is black and he has black spots on his paws too.

Coyote &
The Mice

Have you ever heard Coyote laugh? They say there is a simple way to make him laugh. All you have to do is call him by a certain name. So it's easy. That is, if you can remember the name.

Once there was a whole tribe of mice living in the tall grass near a spring. They had a good life. There was plenty of water to drink and the tender grass shoots were good to eat. Bushes growing nearby gave them leaves and sticks to make their nests with.

But the mice had a problem. Everytime they went down to the water to drink, Coyote would appear and chase them back down their holes. He hardly ever caught one—they were too quick. But it was a nuisance being chased around by Coyote.

So one day the mice held a council to discuss what might be done about Coyote. The Mouse Chief stood up and spoke. "I think we should play a trick on Coyote and teach him a lesson."

The mice all scratched their heads and tried to think of a trick. Then the Mouse Chief got an idea. "Let me see," he mused. "There was a way to make Coyote laugh. My father told me about it. It was a name you could call him. Now, what was that name?"

The Mouse Chief thought and thought but couldn't remember. He went from mouse to mouse asking, "Do you remember the name...? Do *you* remember the name...?"

They all shook their heads. But finally one little mouse piped up, "Yellow-Behind-The-Ears!"

"That's it!" cried the Mouse Chief. "Yellow-Behind-The-Ears!" And then he told his plan.

He said that the next morning all the mice should hide themselves in the grass beside the trail. When Coyote came to get water, the Mouse Chief would give the signal, and they would all holler *Yellow-Behind-The-Ears* and make Coyote laugh.

But the other mice said, "But why do we want to make Coyote laugh?"

The Mouse Chief reminded them that Coyote had a den nearby, where he had a wife and several babies. Every morning Coyote filled his mouth with water to take home for his family. They had all seen him do it. "But," the Mouse Chief chuckled, "can he carry water in his mouth and laugh at the same time?"

The mice all giggled. Now they understood what a good trick it would be.

So the next morning all the mice were hiding in the grass alongside the path Coyote would take to the spring.

Coyote came down to the water. First he drank deeply to quench his own thirst. Then he filled his mouth with water until his cheeks bulged and started back up the trail toward home.

He had hardly started up the trail, when the Mouse Chief scurried to the top of a little pile of dirt and gave the signal.

"Yellow-Behind-The-Ears!" shouted all the mice together.

Coyote laughed — "Hee-hee-hee-ho-ho-ho-ho!" And he spit his water all over the ground.

"Who said that?" Coyote snapped and looked around him. But the mice were hiding back down their holes.

Coyote walked back to the spring, looking carefully about him as he went. And he filled his mouth again with water.

The Mouse Chief let him get a little farther up the trail this time. Then he ran to the dirt mound and gave the signal.

"Yellow-Behind-The-Ears!"

"Hee-hee-hee-ho-ho-ho-ho-ha-ha! *Who said that?*" Coyote darted this way and that. Then he called out a warning, "Remember! I am Coyote. If you say that again, I'll eat you!"

Coyote walked cautiously back to the spring, turning his head to the left and to the right. He filled his cheeks and turned around slowly. He said to himself, "I don't care if they say it again. This time I won't laugh."

The Mouse Chief let Coyote get half way up the hill at the spring's edge. Then he signaled.

"Yellow-Behind-The-Ears!"

Coyote squeezed his lips together. His eyes bulged and he snorted and sputtered as he tried to hold his laughter.

But—"Hee-hee-hee-ho-ho-ho-ho-ha-ha-ha-ha!" He laughed louder than ever.

"*Who said that?*" Coyote roared. He ran from bush to bush sniffing and digging with his paws. He poked his nose behind each clump of grass. But the mice were safe in their holes giggling to themselves.

Coyote crept back to the water. His ears were pricked. His eyes scanned slowly about him. His nose twitched as he scented the wind.

Slowly he filled his mouth, raising his head to look around at each sip. Then he spun and ran up the trail as fast as he could.

The Mouse Chief let him get almost to the top of the hill. And then...

"Yellow-Behind-The-Ears!"

Coyote hooted—"Hee-hee-hee-ho-ho-ho-ho-ha-ha-ha-ha!" Then a thought struck Coyote.

"Ghosts! It must be ghosts!" And Coyote was afraid of ghosts. He ran off howling, "Ghooooooooooooosts... Ghooooooooooooooooosts!"

When he arrived home without any water, his wife was furious. She sent him away again. He had to run clear around the mountain to the next spring to get water for his family. And that's where Coyote went for water from that day on.

So now the mice could go down to drink whenever
they pleased. They would sit back on their haunches
and let the the cool water trickle down their throats.
And sometimes the Mouse Chief would get a little twinkle
in his eye—and then give the signal. The mice would all
shout, "Yellow-Behind-The-Ears!" And they would laugh
even harder than Coyote!

Coyote &
Locust

There was once a locust who made his home on the bank of an arroyo, where it was nice and cool and moist.

Nearby there was a big piñon tree. That was where he liked to go to sing.

One sunny morning the locust felt so good, he just had to sing! He flew up into the tree and began his song:

```
     zz          zz          zz                    zz          zz          zz
  zz  zz      zz  zz      zz  zz            zz  zz      zz  zz      zz  zz
Zz        zzzz        zzzz        zzzz... Zz        zzzz        zzzz        zzzz...
```

Coyote came running by and he heard the song. He stopped and looked up. "Locust," he said, "you sing beautifully. Teach me your song!"

Now the locust didn't like Coyote too well. You know, coyotes eat insects when they're hungry enough. But the locust thought it wouldn't hurt to sing just once. So he sang:

```
   ZZ         ZZ         ZZ              ZZ        ZZ         ZZ
   ZZ  ZZ     ZZ  ZZ     ZZ  ZZ         ZZ  ZZ    ZZ  ZZ     ZZ  ZZ
Zz         ZZZZ       ZZZZ       ZZZZ ... Zz       ZZZZ      ZZZZ      ZZZZ ...
```

And Coyote started singing. But he couldn't sing very well. He growled and howled:

```
   RR         RR                  OO                   OO
   RR  RR     RR  RR          OO  OO             OO  OO
RR         RRRR       RRRR ... OO       OOOO ... OO        OOOO ...
```

"Locust!" Coyote cried. "Did you hear me? I did it!"
"Wellll," Locust buzzed, "that was almost right."
So Coyote started for home. As he ran along he sang:

```
   RR         RR                  OO                   OO
   RR  RR     RR  RR          OO  OO             OO  OO
RR         RRRR       RRRR ... OO       OOOO ... OO        OOOO ...
```

"Oh!" Coyote said to himself, "When I get home, I'll sing this song for my children. They can dance to it before they go to sleep!" He threw his head back and sang even louder.

But there was a prairie dog up ahead, and he saw Coyote running along singing his head off. So Prairie Dog decided to make a trap for

Coyote. He dug a deep hole in the middle of the trail Coyote was running along.

Here came Coyote with his head thrown back, singing at the top of his voice. *Crash!* Coyote fell into the hole.

Coyote got up coughing and sniffing and rubbing the dirt from his eyes. Then, when he'd settled back down, he raised his head to sing again. But he had forgotten the song!

"Oh, well," Coyote said. "I'll get Locust to sing it again." So he ran back to the tree.

"Locust," Coyote called up. "That good-for-nothing Prairie Dog dug a hole in the trail, and I fell in and forgot your song. Sing it for me again."

The locust was getting tired of Coyote bothering him. But Coyote grinned up, showing his teeth, and Locust knew he'd better sing. So he began:

```
     ZZ          ZZ          ZZ              ZZ          ZZ          ZZ
   ZZ  ZZ      ZZ  ZZ      ZZ  ZZ          ZZ  ZZ      ZZ  ZZ      ZZ  ZZ
Zz       ZZZZ        ZZZZ        ZZZZ... Zz       ZZZZ        ZZZZ        ZZZZ...
```

And Coyote started up again:

```
     RR          RR                  OO                  OO
   RR  RR      RR  RR              OO  OO              OO  OO
RR       RRRR        RRRR... OO         OOOO... OO         OOOO...
```

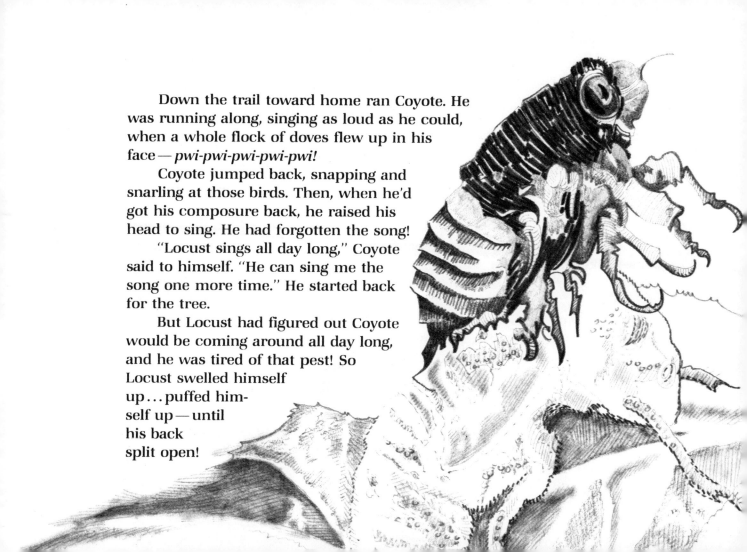

Down the trail toward home ran Coyote. He was running along, singing as loud as he could, when a whole flock of doves flew up in his face—*pwi-pwi-pwi-pwi-pwi!*

Coyote jumped back, snapping and snarling at those birds. Then, when he'd got his composure back, he raised his head to sing. He had forgotten the song!

"Locust sings all day long," Coyote said to himself. "He can sing me the song one more time." He started back for the tree.

But Locust had figured out Coyote would be coming around all day long, and he was tired of that pest! So Locust swelled himself up...puffed himself up—until his back split open!

Locust climbed out of his skin. Then he walked down the tree to the ground. He found a piece of hard, white rock. He brought the rock back up the tree and put it inside the old skin. Then he closed the skin up and sealed it with some sap from the tree. He flew down to his home.

Coyote got back to the tree and said, "Locust! Those worthless doves flew right up in my face, and I forgot your song again. Sing it one more time!"

Of course nothing happened. It was just a skin with a rock in it that Coyote was talking to. But Coyote called up, "Locust! Didn't you hear me? I said sing me your song!"

Still nothing happened. And Coyote started to get angry. "Locust," he warned, "I'm going to ask you four more times — and that's all!"

"Once...Sing me your song." Nothing happened.

"Twice, Locust...Sing me your song!" Still nothing.

"Locust, do you see my teeth...? Sing me your song...

"LOCUST! If you don't want to get eaten, you had better *sing me your song!*"

When nothing happened, Coyote jumped up and snipped the locust off the branch and bit it hard!

"OOOoooowwwwwwwwwwwwwwww..." He ran off howling. His teeth were all broken and crushed and pushed back into his jaws.

Coyote ran until he came to a stream. Then he lapped up the cool water to ease the pain in his mouth.

Then, when he looked at his reflection in the water, he saw the same thing you will ever see if you ever look into a coyote's mouth. The front teeth are long and straight and white. But the side teeth in a coyote's mouth are all stumpy and crooked and look as if they've been driven back into his jaws.

That's because long ago a coyote bit a rock, thinking he would eat a locust.

And if you go walking around in the summertime, you'll see that the locust still climbs out of his skin and leaves his empty shell on the branches of a tree. He does that to fool the coyotes that want to eat him!

Coyote &
The Rock

Once Coyote and Fox went walking together. They came to a big, smooth rock. Coyote spread his blanket over it and together they sat down on the rock and smoked their pipes.

When they stood up to go, Coyote looked down at the rock and said, "What a nice rock this is! I think I'll give it my blanket. My blanket will keep this good rock warm and dry."

Then Coyote walked off with Fox, leaving his blanket behind covering the rock. They walked on down the hillside toward the river. But they hadn't gone far when dark clouds gathered above and a cold rain began to fall.

Coyote hugged himself and shivered. *"Brrrr!* Now I wish I still had my blanket." And he told Fox, "Run back and tell Rock I want to borrow my blanket for a while."

Fox ran off up the hill, but he returned without the blanket. "Rock wouldn't let me have it," he told Coyote. "He says it's his and he wants to use it."

That made Coyote angry. "That selfish rock!" he muttered. And he ran back up the hill and jerked the blanket off Rock.

"Rock," Coyote growled, "you've been lying here in the sun and rain for a thousand summers and winters. It wouldn't hurt you to get a few more raindrops on you. I only wanted to borrow my blanket for a short time to keep dry. Now I'm taking my blanket back. You can lie here uncovered for the rest of time!"

Coyote threw his blanket around himself and Fox and they continued their walk down the hill.

Soon the sun came back out and Coyote and Fox sat down again to talk. But just when they sat down, they heard a strange noise above them — *a-thump-thump-thump-thump* — *a-thump-thump-thump-thump*.

"Fox," Coyote said, "run up the hill and see what is making that noise."

Fox disappeared over the crest of the hill, but he soon reappeared, running as fast as he could, with his tail stretched out behind him. "Coyote!" Fox barked, "Run for your life! The rock is after us!"

Fox dived into a badger hole, but his tail didn't quite make it out of the way. Rock rolled over the tip of Fox's tail and to this day it has been white.

Coyote turned and dashed toward the river. He leaped into the water and swam to the other side. Coyote shook himself and sat down on the bank to rest. He knew the rock would sink if it tried to cross the river after him.

Imagine Coyote's surprise when he saw the rock roll into the river and begin to swim across — *a-blub-blub-blub-blub* — *a-blub-blub-blub-blub.*

Coyote ran into a thick forest. Surely the trees would stop Rock. He reached the center of the forest and paused to catch his breath. Coyote heard a terrible crashing and

thundering as Rock toppled the trees and knocked them to splinters. And on it came — *a-thump-thump-thump-thump* — *a-thump-thump-thump-thump.*

Coyote ran toward the prairie at the far side of the forest. When he reached the edge of the trees, he met Bear.

"Bear!" Coyote panted. "Please help me. A rock is after me!"

Bear roared, *"Waaaahhh!* I'll swat that rock with my paw!"

Bear sat down to wait, and when Rock came past, he swung his paw. *"Aaaooouuuuu!"* Bear rocked back clutching his broken paw against his chest.

The rock rolled on — *a-thump-thump-thump-thump* — *a-thump-thump-thump-thump*.

Coyote ran across the prairie, and he saw Buffalo grazing on some green grass. "Buffalo!" Coyote begged. "Please help me. A rock is after me."

Buffalo snorted, "I'll butt that rock with my head!" And Buffalo lowered his head and charged at the rock. They met — *boom!* Buffalo flew through the air. His horns were broken and his head split open.

And the rock rolled on — *a-thump-thump-thump-thump* — *a-thump-thump-thump-thump*.

Coyote ran and ran. Now the rock was right at his heels — *thump-thump-thump*. He saw a lodge ahead of him, and standing near it were two old women with stone hatchets in their hands. The women called to him, "Run between us, Coyote. Run between us!"

Coyote did. And when the rock passed between the old women, they lowered their hatchets — *crack!* The rock shattered into a thousand pieces.

Coyote lay on the ground with his heart pounding, panting for his breath. The old women walked to the other side of the lodge and whispered to each other. But Coyote could hear what they were saying.

"How nice and fat Coyote is," the old women whispered. "He'll make a fine meal for us."

Then Coyote knew the old women were witches. He'd better plan his escape. He saw some jugs of water beside the lodge and he crept over and dumped the water out.

When the old women returned, Coyote said, "I'm thirsty from that long run. Could I have a drink of water?"

They said, "Certainly. Drink from one of those jugs over there."

Coyote walked over to the jugs. "These are all empty," he told them. "But that's all right. I'll take one down to the river and fill it."

Coyote picked up a jug and walked off. As soon as he was sure the women couldn't see him, he threw the jug to the ground and ran away laughing to himself.

When Coyote didn't come back, the witches realized that he had tricked them. They began to argue, each one accusing the other of letting Coyote escape.

Finally, they grew so angry they picked up their stone hatchets and hit one another over the head. And that was the end of those witches. And it's the end of the story too.

But not the end of Coyote. He had many more adventures.

Coyote &
Bluebird

The old stories tell us that in the time long ago, not all things were as they are now. The cardinal was just as red as he is today. And the meadow lark had his yellow shirt and black necklace. But the bird we know as the bluebird was a dusty brown color. And what about Coyote? He was bright green!

One day Bluebird went to a medicine man and complained about his color. "Look at me," he sulked. "The dirt is as pretty as I am. Isn't there some way for me to change the way I look?"

And the medicine man told Bluebird about a spring that was four days' journey to the west. It had no stream running into it nor running out of it, because its water welled up from deep within the earth, where the gods lived. Its color was deep blue, the blue of the mountain sky on a bright afternoon in winter.

The medicine man said that if Bluebird would bathe in that spring each morning for four days and sing a certain song, his feathers would become the color of the water.

And so Bluebird traveled westward for four days and found the spring. Each morning he bathed in its water and sang the song the medicine man had taught him.

The first morning he came from the water with feathers the gray-blue of the dawn sky. After his second bath, he was the color of the sky at mid-morning. On the third morning his feathers deepened to the blue of the noonday sky.

On the fourth morning when Bluebird flew up from the water, he was the deep blue of the mountain sky on a bright afternoon in winter!

Bluebird flew to the top of a nearby tree and sang out his joy. And who should come wandering by, but Coyote.

Coyote recognized the song he was hearing and looked up expecting to see a dusty brown bird. Instead, he saw the most beautiful blue bird he had ever seen. Coyote was jealous.

"Bluebird," Coyote called, "how did you get so beautiful?"

Bluebird told Coyote exactly what the medicine man had told him. He even taught Coyote the song.

Coyote ran to the spring and bathed, singing as Bluebird taught him.

He climbed out and shook himself, and his green fur was a pale gray-blue.

The next day, Coyote bathed and sang again, and the same on the third and fourth mornings, until he was the same rich blue as the Bluebird.

Coyote was so proud of himself! He ran off to show the other animals how beautiful he had grown.

Then, as Coyote ran along, he had a thought. He wondered if his shadow was blue too. He turned to look, and didn't see a low ledge in front of him.

Coyote ran right off the ledge and tumbled over and over in the soft dirt below. The dirt stuck to Coyote's wet fur.

When Coyote stood up, he was the color of the dirt—a dull grayish brown. And that's the color he has been to this day.

Coyote &
The Blackbirds

Everyone knows that each animal has its own way of acting. Rabbits behave as rabbits should. Mice act like mice, deer like deer. Then there is Coyote. He always wants to do the things other animals do.

One autumn day Coyote was wandering along the side of a mountain, sniffing the air and twitching his whiskers, when he heard a high-pitched singing.

Coyote hurried to find out who was making the music and he came upon the blackbirds doing their autumn ceremonial dances. Every year, before flying south, the blackbirds come together for a day of dancing. Coyote knew that. But he had never seen their dance before.

Coyote watched the birds, and he thought he had never seen finer dances in his life. Row after row of blackbirds danced down the mountainside, whirling and hopping and flapping their wings. Then they rose into the air and flew in a great circle, landing back where they had begun.

Coyote admired the dancers for a while. Then a thought struck him — he could dance like that. He was sure he could — all but the last part, anyway.

So Coyote trotted over to the Blackbird Chief. "Please let me join in your beautiful dance," he begged. "This is the finest dance I have ever seen."

"No, Coyote," the chief told him, turning his head this way and that. "This is a blackbird dance, not a coyote dance."

"Please," Coyote begged. "Just let me try it once. I've been watching you and I'm sure I can do it."

Coyote asked a third time, and a fourth. And finally the chief agreed to let Coyote join the dance.

Coyote fell in with a line of dancers and went whirling and leaping down the slope. He flailed his arms about as if they were wings.

At the bottom of the hill, the birds rose up and flew away. Coyote sat watching them go. He wrinkled his brow and cocked his head as he studied the birds wheeling above him.

Then another thought struck. He ran back to the chief. "Did you see me?" he pestered. "Did you see me? I told you I knew the dance."

"Well, that was fairly good—for a Coyote," the chief admitted.

"Thank you," Coyote panted. "Now I have an even better idea. I think I could do the last part too—if you birds would only lend me some feathers."

The chief studied Coyote with first one eye, then the other.

Coyote pleaded, "You birds have plenty of feathers. Couldn't each of you spare just one?"

The Blackbird Chief thought this

might be a chance to teach
Coyote a lesson. He warned
Coyote, "It will hurt when
I attach the feathers."
"What's a little pain?"
Coyote insisted. "Let
me try it."
So the chief
called all the birds
together

and had each one pluck a feather from its wing. Then the chief began poking the feathers into the skin of Coyote's front leg.

Coyote howled every time a quill pierced his skin. "I told you it would hurt," the chief said and went on until Coyote had feathers all along his front legs and down his sides.

Then Coyote hurried to join the dancers. Down the mountainside he twirled. When he flapped his front legs, he could feel the lifting force of the feathers. When they reached the bottom, and the birds flew up, Coyote worked his front legs furiously. Slowly he rose into the air.

Higher and higher flew Coyote. "Look at me! Look at me!" he shouted at the birds as he flapped madly after them. He darted about, unable to control his flight.

Then, just when he thought he had the knack of flying, the feathers began to fall from Coyote's legs. He flapped even faster, but he was steadily falling. *Crash!* Coyote hit the ground and was nearly killed.

"Oooohhh," moaned Coyote as he struggled to his feet, "I guess that's enough dancing for one day." He staggered off, and the blackbirds flew to the south laughing as they went.

And every year, as the flocks of blackbirds fly past on their southward journey, we can hear them laughing about how Coyote tried to act like someone else and ended up making a coyote of himself, as usual.

Coyote &
The Rattlesnake

oyote loved games and contests — especially when he was sure he would win. And there was nothing he liked better than making fun of some animal he thought was weaker than himself.

Once when Coyote was loping along through the desert, he saw Rattlesnake making his way from one shady bush to another. Coyote sat down and watched the snake wriggle along.

Finally Coyote spoke. "Snake," he said, "you certainly are a miserable little animal. Why, you're not much bigger around than my leg!"

The rattlesnake didn't answer. He just curled up in the shade of his new bush and watched Coyote with his sharp yellow eyes.

Once Coyote started making fun of someone, he didn't like to stop, so he stepped over closer to the snake to see what other faults he could find.

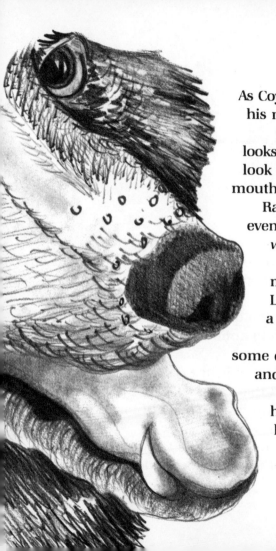

As Coyote approached, Rattlesnake's black tongue darted from his mouth.

Coyote laughed. "Rattlesnake, is that your tongue? It looks like a piece of dead grass. This is what a tongue should look like!" And Coyote hung his long pink tongue from his mouth and panted.

Rattlesnake didn't say a word. But when Coyote came even closer, Rattlesnake raised his tail and shook it— *wwhhhrrr!*

Coyote howled with glee. "Is that the music you make? It sounds like a bean pod shaking in the wind. Listen to this!" Coyote threw his head back and sent out a high, wavering song. "Now *that's* music!"

Coyote felt so superior to Rattlesnake that he kicked some dirt in the snake's face. Rattlesnake arched his neck and opened his mouth.

Now Coyote nearly fell over laughing. "Rattlesnake," he sputtered, "you have only two teeth! Oh! You poor little weakling!"

Coyote drew his lips back from his teeth. "See what a fine set of teeth I have."

Then a thought entered Coyote's mind. Maybe he could get a meal out of this—not a very good one, but there was some meat on that skinny old snake. "I could bite that snake in two," Coyote thought. "It would hardly make a mark if Rattlesnake bit me!"

So Coyote said, "Rattlesnake, let's play a game. We'll bite one another and see which one hurts the most."

Still Rattlesnake didn't speak. He just followed Coyote with his beady eyes.

"What's the matter, Rattlesnake?" Coyote wheedled. "Don't you like games? Let me show you how much fun they can be!" And Coyote jumped forward and bit Rattlesnake in the middle of his body.

Rattlesnake whipped his head around and sunk his fangs into Coyote's shoulder.

"Yipe!" Coyote jumped back. That had hurt more than he thought it would. But Coyote could see a dent in the middle of Rattlesnake's body where his jaws had closed, and little drops of blood showed where his teeth had pierced the snake's skin.

Coyote pretended to be cheerful. "There, Rattlesnake. Wasn't that fun? Now you just stay there under your bush. I'll lie down under this one and we'll see how we feel in a little while."

Coyote lay down thinking the snake would surely die before long. And he was sure the burning pain in his shoulder would soon go away. After all, the bite was made with just two teeth.

But the pain spread all over Coyote's body. His head was swimming. "Snake," Coyote called out, "how do you feel?" There was no answer. "Oooooo," Coyote groaned, "I don't feel very well at all."

When the sun set and the air cooled off, Rattlesnake went on his way. But Coyote lay under that bush for four days before he was well enough to walk again.

Coyote recovered from the snake bite. But ever since that day, when Coyote sees a rattlesnake, he doesn't say a word. And he certainly doesn't offer to play any games!

Coyote & Turtle

Did you know that turtles are very brave animals? If you stop to think, you'll see they are. They never run away—not even from their fiercest enemies. And they certainly aren't afraid of Coyote.

One fine day in spring the turtles all decided to leave their home in the river and hunt for tender green cactus shoots. They all moved slowly up the river bank and out onto the desert, but Little Turtle, the youngest of the clan, moved slowest of all.

Little Turtle had never been out of the river before and this new world was fascinating to him. He stopped to investigate each colorful rock or bush or clump of grass. His mother kept calling for him to hurry and catch up.

Then Little Turtle saw a patch of blue flowers. He wandered over to see them more closely, and when he looked up he realized that he was all alone.

Now, as I said, turtles are very brave, but this turtle was so young and this place was so strange that he began to cry—"*hoo-hoo-hoo*"—and turned to go home.

Little Turtle started back toward the river sobbing softly to himself, and who should happen by but Coyote. Coyote sat down and cocked his ear toward Little Turtle. Finally Coyote said, "Little Turtle, what a fine song you're singing!

"I'm not singing," Little Turtle pouted. "I'm crying! Don't you know the difference between singing and crying?"

Coyote paid no attention. "Yes," he went on, "I know good music when I hear it. That is a fine song. Sing it a little louder for me."

"I told you I'm not singing. *I'm crying!*"

Now Coyote grew impatient. "Little Turtle, if you don't sing me your song good and loud, I'll swallow you whole."

That would be enough to frighten any other animal Little Turtle's size, but Little Turtle's mother had told him about Coyote. He knew what to do. He told Coyote, "Go on—swallow me. I'll bounce around in your stomach like a stone and kill you."

Coyote reached out a paw and touched Little Turtle's shell. It was hard as stone.

"Well, then," Coyote said, "I'll jump on you with all four feet and crush you!"

"Go ahead and try it. My shell is strong. It won't hurt me a bit. My mother told me so."

"What if I throw you against a rock?"

"The rock will break," Little Turtle said. "I won't feel a thing. My mother told me only one thing can hurt me."

Now Coyote changed his tone. "Really?" he praised. "How strong you are! Only one thing can hurt you? Let me guess what it is: It must be Mountain Lion's sharp claws."

Little Turtle laughed, "Mountain Lion's claws will break on my shell."

"Then maybe it's Bear's powerful jaws?"

"Bear might as well try to crush a rock with his jaws. My shell will be harder."

"I give up, Little Turtle. Tell me what it is."

"My mother said that nothing can hurt me but the cold water of the river." Little Turtle shivered. "Oouuu! I hate cold water!"

Now Coyote laughed. "You foolish turtle. Since you hate water so much, that's just where I'll throw you!" And he picked Little Turtle up in his mouth and ran to the river and threw him into the water.

Little Turtle poked his head out of the water laughing. "Thank you, Coyote," he called out. "The river is where I live. You saved me a long walk back home." And Little Turtle swam away.

Coyote was so angry that he started to cry — "*Howw-ow-ow-ow...*"

A raven in a nearby tree heard Coyote and called down to him, "*Caw!* Coyote, what a beautiful song you're singing!! *Caw!*"

"Stupid bird!" Coyote screamed, "don't you know the difference between singing and crying?"

Coyote &
The Quail

All the other birds used to make fun of the quail. They called them clumsy and cowardly. For one thing, quail can't fly very well. It's true Roadrunner can't fly well either—but Roadrunner kills rattlesnakes. You have to admire that kind of courage. Quail seem to spend most of their time running away from something. A lot of the time, it's Coyote.

One day Coyote had had a good meal of field mice. He was full, and he lay down under a bush and went to sleep.

While Coyote slept, a covey of quail came marching past. They twittered and trembled. "Look!" they whispered back and forth. "There is our enemy, Coyote."

The quail were frightened, but Coyote looked so harmless as he lay with his eyes closed and his nose twitching flies away that they didn't run off.

Then one of the bravest quail spoke. "Let's pay Coyote back for all the trouble he's caused us," the brave quail said. "We'll never have a better chance."

The other quail grew wide-eyed at the idea. But the brave quail ran up and plucked a hair—*plip!*—from Coyote's tail with his beak. He scurried back to the covey while the other quail chuckled.

Seeing the brave quail made the others feel stronger. A second ran up and—*plip!*—snatched another hair from Coyote's tail. Then another did it, and another—*plip! plip! plip!*

Soon there wasn't a hair left in Coyote's tail. It was as bare as a winter branch. The quail ran off giggling to themselves.

In a little while Coyote woke up. He yawned and stretched his front legs and then set out trotting across the desert without looking behind. Coyote held his tail up high, as he always did when he felt happy.

As he went on his way, Coyote passed the quail hiding in some tall grass. When they saw the bald tail Coyote so proudly carried behind him, the quail all giggled — *hee-hee-hee!*

Coyote stopped. "What are you laughing at?" he demanded.

"Who, us?" called back the brave quail. "We weren't laughing. A bee must have buzzed in your ear."

Coyote turned and trotted on. But he looked so funny, the quail couldn't hold their laughter — *hee-hee-hee!*

Coyote spun around. "Why are you laughing?" he shouted.

"No one laughed," the brave quail told him. "Maybe the wind is blowing through the trees."

Coyote ran on without looking back. He had gone quite a distance before he happened to pass a prickly pear cactus. Normally, Coyote could brush against a cactus and his fur would let him slip smoothly across the needles without getting stuck. But this time the spines dug deep into the skin of his bare tail.

Coyote yipped and jumped away from the cactus. Then he looked around to see why his hair hadn't protected him.

For the first time, Coyote saw his bare tail. He raised his head and howled furiously. Then he remembered the quail. So that's what they were laughing at!

Coyote ran back to the tall grass, and when the quail saw him coming, they scattered in terror. Coyote chased them this way and that, until their poor wings were tired from so much flying. And running on the ground, they were no match for Coyote's speed.

Just then the brave quail spotted a deserted rabbit hole. He called out to his cousins, "Follow me!" And as the brave quail led the way to the hole, he snatched up a piece of cholla cactus in his beak. The brave quail scurried down the rabbit hole, and all the other quail followed.

But Coyote was determined to find the culprit who had plucked his tail. He dug away at the hole until the dirt flew in a great cloud behind him.

Coyote reached the first quail and grabbed it by the throat. "Did you pull the hair out of my tail?"

"Oh, no!" the quail sputtered. "It must have been one much braver than I. Maybe it was my cousin who is still in the hole."

Coyote released the trembling quail and dug deeper. He seized another quail. "Did you pull the hair from my tail?"

"Oh, no! It wasn't I. It must have been one much braver than I. Maybe it was my cousin who is still in the hole."

Coyote dug on. From each quail he got the same reply, and so he let each go and dug further. Finally he reached the brave quail. "Did you pluck my tail?"

"No!" the brave quail lied. "It must have been this brave quail that is still in the hole behind me." He pointed over his shoulder at the cholla cactus joint which lay at the very bottom of the hole. In the darkness the rough skin of the cactus did look like bird feathers.

Coyote let the brave quail go and shouted down the hole, "Did you pull the hair from my tail?"

There was no answer, and Coyote thought, "So you're afraid to speak. You must be the guilty one!"

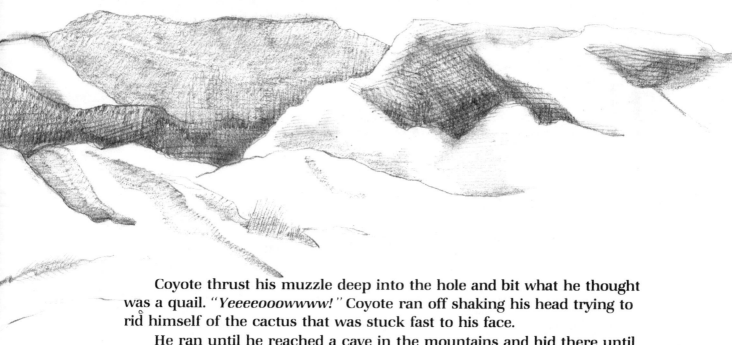

Coyote thrust his muzzle deep into the hole and bit what he thought was a quail. *"Yeeeeooowwww!"* Coyote ran off shaking his head trying to rid himself of the cactus that was stuck fast to his face.

He ran until he reached a cave in the mountains and hid there until one by one the thorns dropped from his mouth. And in that time he had grown a fine bushy tail.

All the while Coyote was gone, the quail had lived in peace. And afterward, even if they did have to run from Coyote again, at least they didn't have to put up with any more teasing from the other birds. Not even Roadrunner had ever played such a fine trick on Coyote!

Coyote &
Horned Toad

One year Horned Toad planted a garden. He dug up the soil and smoothed it with a stick. And then he went along planting the seeds. As he worked he sang softly to himself. Coyote heard that song and, as usual, he had to investigate.

"What are you doing?" Coyote demanded, without so much as saying a polite hello.

Now, Horned Toad didn't like Coyote one little bit. Coyote was always picking on members of the horned toad tribe. So Horned Toad went on with his work without answering.

Of course Coyote was very offended. "Horned Toad, don't you have any manners? I asked you what you're doing."

Horned Toad didn't even look up. He just went on planting seeds.

Now Coyote was angry. "Horned Toad, if you don't answer me, I'll swallow you whole!"

"I'm too fat for that," Horned Toad hissed, still not looking up. "You can't swallow me whole, and you know it."

"Is that so?" growled Coyote. "Just watch!" And with that Coyote took Horned Toad in his mouth and, sure enough, swallowed him in one gulp.

Coyote jogged off chuckling to himself. He didn't know that he had done just what Horned Toad wanted. As he rode along inside Coyote, Horned Toad began to sing his song again.

Coyote stopped and listened. "Who is singing?" Coyote asked, looking all around him.

Horned Toad squeaked, "I am." And he went on with his song.

Coyote spun around in circles. He looked up in the air and down between his feet. "Where are you?" he demanded.

"Right here."

"Where?"

"Here," Horned Toad called out. And he thumped his foot.

"Ouch!" yipped Coyote. Then he realized what was happening. "Horned Toad," Coyote pleaded, "come out of there. You're going to hurt something."

But Horned Toad told him, "Don't hurry me, Coyote. This is very interesting. I've never seen a coyote's insides before. I'm in a very strange place right now."

"What does it look like?" Coyote asked.

"It's all wrinkled and full of the strangest mixture of food—berries and mice and grasshoppers."

"That's my breakfast you're seeing. You're in my stomach. If you hurt it, I'll never enjoy a meal again. Come up out of there."

Horned Toad hopped twice, and then said, "Look at this!"

Coyote winced. "What do you see?"

"It's red and soft and shiny."

"That's my liver. I couldn't live if my liver were damaged. Be careful!"

Horned Toad hopped again.

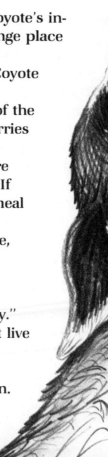

"Ho! What's this thing?"

"Tell me what it looks like," Coyote gasped.

"It's round like a stream rock. And it's leaping about."

"It's MY HEART!"Coyote screamed. "Stay away from it. If you so much as touch it, I'll surely die!"

But Horned Toad was in no mood to be kind to Coyote. He raised one of his spiked hind feet and kicked Coyote's heart.

Coyote groaned and fell to the ground. He stretched out his legs and lay still. Horned Toad hopped out of his mouth and went back to his garden.

Some say that Coyote died. But others say that Coyote carries the secret to his life in a safer place than his heart and that he returned to life again. Whichever is true, I don't think Coyote ever bothered Horned Toad any more.

BIBLIOGRAPHY

Benedict, Ruth. *Tales of the Cochiti Indians*. Smithsonian Institution Bureau
of American Ethnology Bulletin 98, 1931.

Coffin, Tristam P., editor. *Indian Tales of North America: An Anthology for the
Adult Reader*. American Folk-lore Society Bibliographical and Special
Series 13. Austin: University of Texas Press, 1961.

Cushing, Frank Hamilton. *Zuni Folk Tales*. New York: G.P. Putnam & Sons,
1901.

de Huff, Elizabeth Willis. *Taytay's Memories*. New York: Harcourt, Brace & Co.,
1924.

Goodwin, Grenville. *Tales of the White Mountain Apache*. Memoirs, 33. New
York: American Folklore Society, 1939.

Hogner, Dorothy Childs. *Navajo Winter Nights*. New York: E.M. Hale & Co., 1935.

McKee, Louis & Summers, Richard. *Dusty Desert Tales*. Caldwell: The Caxton
Printers, Ltd., 1941.

Parsons, Elsie Clews. *Tewa Tales*. Memoirs, 19. New York: American Folk-Lore
Society, 1926.

_____ . *Taos Tales*. Memoirs, 34. New York: American Folk-
Lore Society, 1940.

THE ILLUSTRATOR

Lucy Jelinek is an artist-designer who has worked in New Mexico since 1978. Her company, Santa Fe Pre-Print, is a graphic design firm specializing in publications. She also designed and illustrated Joe Hayes' first collection of stories, *The Day It Snowed Tortillas*.

THE PUBLISHER

Mariposa Printing & Publishing was established in 1980. Our goal is to provide quality commercial printing to the Santa Fe community and to provide quality-crafted, limited edition publications in various literary fields.

Titles include *Opening* by Malcolm Brown, *The Day It Snowed Tortillas* and *Coyote &* by Joe Hayes, and *Sweet Salt*, a novel by Robert Mayer.

Your comments and suggestions are appreciated. Contact Joe Mowrey, owner-production manager, Mariposa Printing & Publishing, 922 Baca Street, Santa Fe, New Mexico, (505) 988-5582.